This Little Tiger book belongs to:

_____

_____

_____

_____

For Doris and George
~*A.H.B.*

For Matthew and Sally
~*J.C.*

First published in Great Britain 1996 as *What if?*
This paperback edition published in 2003 by
LITTLE TIGER PRESS
An imprint of Magi Publications
1 The Coda Centre, 189 Munster Road, London SW6 6AW
www.littletigerpress.com

Text copyright © A.H.Benjamin 1996
Illustrations copyright © Jane Chapman 1996
A.H.Benjamin and Jane Chapman have asserted their rights
to be identified as the author and illustrator of this work under
the Copyright, Designs and Patents Act, 1988.

BAA! MOO!
WHAT WILL WE DO?

A.H. BENJAMIN and JANE CHAPMAN

LITTLE TIGER PRESS
London

Something special was happening on Buttercup Farm. The farmer had brought a kangaroo back with him from Australia. It was arriving that very day! All the animals gathered in the farmyard to talk about it. They had never seen a kangaroo before.

"What can a kangaroo do,
anyway?" they asked.
But nobody knew.

"What if she can crow?" asked Rooster. "What if she gets up very early and crows so loudly that she wakes the whole farm? Perhaps she will even count the hens and chicks to see if any are missing. The farmer won't need me any more then, and I will have to look for another job.
Cock-a-doodle-doo!
Perhaps I won't even find one!"

"How dreadful!"
said everyone.

"What if she can herd sheep?" said Dog.
"What if she rounds them all up, and takes
them to graze on the highest and greenest
hills? She might even chase a fox or two.
The farmer will be so pleased with her that
he will send me off to live in the kennels.
Bow-wow!
I would hate that!"

"How horrible!"

said everyone.

"What if she can catch mice?" said Cat.
"What if she catches all the mice in the barn
and a few rats, too? Maybe even the spiders
would be scared to live there. Then the
farmer would get rid of me,
and I would become a stray,
foraging for food in dustbins.
Miaow!

I'd miss my milk and sardines!"

"What if she can give milk?" said Cow. "What if she fills up all the churns in the farm with such rich, creamy milk that people will rush to buy it? Then nobody would want mine, and the farmer would make me pull the heavy plough instead. *Moo!*

I couldn't stand that!"

"**How shocking!**"

said everyone.

"What if she can grow wool?" said Sheep.
"What if she has a thick, woolly fleece,
whiter than snow and softer than silk?
And maybe her coat will grow twice as fast
as mine. The farmer would be so delighted
that my wool would only be used to stuff
old pillows and cushions.
Baa!
I wouldn't let them come near me with
their shears!"

"What if she can pull a cart?" said Horse.
"What if she takes a cartful of fruit and
vegetables to the market and gets there a lot
quicker than I could? She might even give
rides to the farmer's children.
There would be no place for me here then,
and I would end up in an old horses' home.
Neigh! I'm too young for that!"

"How frightful!"

said everyone.

The animals were very, very worried.

They were so busy worrying they did not notice that some of the young ones had strayed away.

"Where are my puppies?" asked Dog, looking around.

"And my kittens?" asked Cat.
Sheep could not find her tiny lamb, either.

All the animals searched and
searched, but not a kitten,
nor a puppy, nor a tiny lamb
could they find anywhere.
They looked from the barn . . .

. . . to the pigsty, with no luck.

"This is dreadful!" crowed Rooster.

"Horrible!" woofed Dog.

"Awful!" miaowed Cat.

"Shocking!" mooed Cow.

"Terrible!" baaed Sheep.

"Frightful!" neighed Horse.

Suddenly, across the field they saw . . .

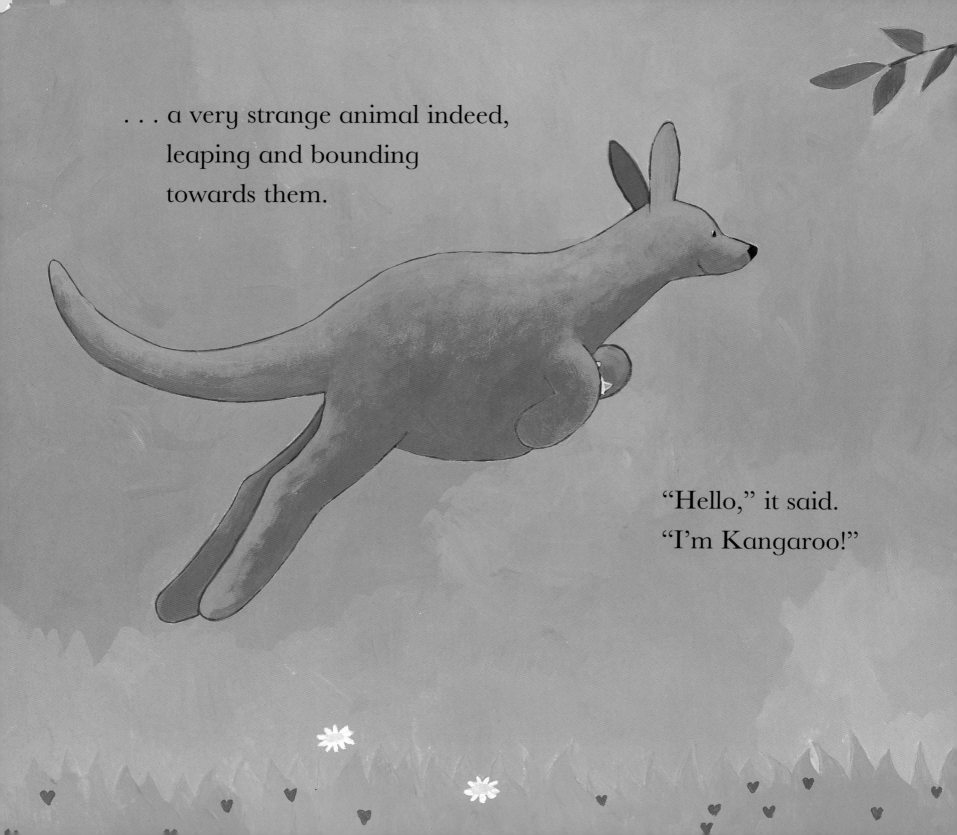

. . . a very strange animal indeed,
leaping and bounding
towards them.

"Hello," it said.
"I'm Kangaroo!"

The animals stopped searching
for their babies.
They stared and stared.
For the funny-looking animal
had a big pouch in her tummy,
and in the pouch . . .

. . . were
three kittens,
two puppies
and
one tiny lamb!

"I've found your babies," said Kangaroo.
"I'm a baby minder. I look after the young,
and carry them when their little feet get tired.
They love it!"
"What a good idea!" the animals cried.
And crowing and barking and miaowing and
mooing and baaing and neighing, they all
welcomed Kangaroo to her new home.

More fantastic books from Little Tiger Press

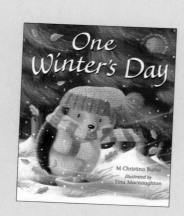

For information regarding any of the above titles or for our catalogue, please contact us:

Little Tiger Press, 1 The Coda Centre,
189 Munster Road, London SW6 6AW, UK
Tel: 020 7385 6333 • Fax: 020 7385 7333
E-mail: info@littletiger.co.uk
www.littletigerpress.com